ADA LOVELACE

CRACKS THE CODE

REBEL GIRLS

Our books are available at special quantity discounts for bulk purchase for sale promotions, premiums, fundraising, and educational needs. For details, write to sales@rebelgirls.co

Text: Corinne Purtill

Cover and Illustrations: Marina Muun

Cover Lettering: Monique Aimee

FSC
www.fsc.org
MIX
Paper from
responsible sources
FSC® C013123

www.rebelgirls.co

ISBN 978-1-7331761-8-7

MORE BOOKS
FROM REBEL GIRLS . . .

Good Night Stories for Rebel Girls

•

Good Night Stories for Rebel Girls 2

•

I Am a Rebel Girl:
A Journal to Start Revolutions

•

Madam C. J. Walker Builds a Business

To the Rebel Girls of the world...

**Grasp your curiosity tightly
and never let go.**

Ada Lovelace

December 10, 1815 - November 27, 1852

England

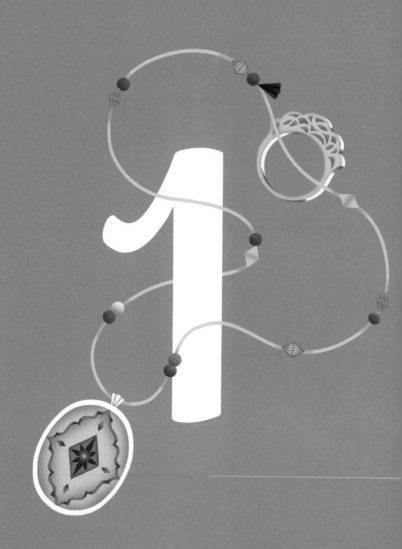

*A*da crept through the jungle, stepping so lightly her shoes made no sound. For weeks, a fearsome tiger had stalked the nearby villages. It devoured people most horribly. And now she, the bravest hunter . . .

No, hunter *wouldn't do. She didn't want to* hurt the tiger.

She, the bravest tiger tamer *(yes, much better) would befriend the animal and convince it to stop eating people. Perhaps it could even be coaxed into living with her as a pet. She gathered her courage, stepped into the clearing, and raised her hands.*

"Got you!" Ada cried, tumbling onto the cushion where her cat, Mistress Puff, had been comfortably napping in a ray of sunlight. Ada

ignored Mistress Puff's yelps of annoyance and snuggled her face into the cat's soft, white fur.

Augusta Ada Byron was eight years old. She lived in a big house just outside of London. It was a good house, with a schoolroom for her lessons and a grand staircase with a huge hall, whose walls made a wonderful, rich sound when you stood on the top step and sang loudly. Sometimes, she pretended the kitchen was a witch's den full of bubbling cauldrons while cackling to herself. (This made the cook shouty and Mama very cross.) Sadly, the things that were most interesting to do and the things that she got scolded for were too often one and the same.

It wasn't that Ada wanted to be naughty. She tried to be a good girl. She wanted to please Mama and her governess, Miss Lamont, who could play the piano and had a lovely Irish accent. But Ada had so much energy that sitting still was simply impossible. One day, she bit the maid who scolded her, and then bit the wooden railing when she was sent to sit on the stairs.

Unfortunately that was the end of Miss Lamont. Since then Ada had taken her lessons from a string of stern-faced tutors. They were good at molding girls into young ladies, she supposed, but not much else.

"Miss Byron!"

Ada jumped, and Puff leapt off her lap and raced down the hallway. All the tutors seemed to know exactly when Ada's mind had wandered. Ada looked enviously after Puff, then hurried to the schoolroom. She looked at the agenda Madame had written on the board: geography, music, French, math, Italian . . . Fifteen minutes at a time until the day was through.

Ada was happy to see geography and music on the day's agenda but much less excited about the math. How was anyone supposed to enjoy a subject without pictures? Geography, on the other hand, was excellent for making up stories.

"Norway is a Scandinavian country with a

rugged coastline and waves as high as seventeen meters—"

"What makes the waves, Madame?" Ada interrupted.

"Hush," Madame replied sternly. "The Norwegian Sea is—"

"Would the waves be taller than our house?"

"Excuse me?"

"The waves. The gardener says that lovely tree in front of our house is fifteen meters high and the tree is taller than the roof. So the waves in Norway would be taller than our house, *n'est-ce pas?* Isn't that so?" Ada looked out the window, imagining the sea swelling across the yard. Water pressed against the glass as if she were a fish inside a tank.

Madame sighed and closed her eyes. She did this often during geography lessons. *Geography must make her sleepy*, Ada thought.

Ada ran her finger along the globe and rested it on Greece. The Greek islands looked like clouds breaking apart to reveal a patch of clear blue sky.

Greece was where her father lived. Mama had told her that the last time she'd asked where her father was. Then Lady Annabella Byron's mouth had grown small and firm which meant Ada was not to ask any more questions.

Ada could not remember meeting her father, though her mother said she had. She kept the presents he had sent her: a ring, a locket, a length of ribbon, and a tiny picture of Italy.

She knew he was a poet, which sounded boring to Ada. All the poetry books she read were full of dull rhymes about children who felt peaceful and good because they listened to their parents. Ada found it hard to imagine any children like that.

She decided instead that her father was a great ship captain. That would explain why he lived in a country surrounded by the sea.

The door swung open, and a woman with brown curls, sharp eyes, and the posture of a queen stepped into the room.

"Mama!"

Instinctively, Ada ran toward her. Then she caught herself at the sight of Lady Byron's fierce expression and stopped to curtsey instead.

"Good morning, Ada," Lady Byron said. "Good morning, Madame. How is Ada's schoolwork?"

"Her French and Italian are excellent, but she is lazy in mathematics and geography. Her daydreams disrupt our lessons."

Ada groaned quietly. Nothing made her mother angrier than daydreaming.

"Ada, I will not have you ruining your education with nonsense and flights of fancy. No more geography and no more stories at bedtime until you focus."

"But Mama . . . "

"That's enough," Annabella scolded, turning to glare at the teacher. "And you, Madame, keep Ada's mischief to a minimum." Annabella left the schoolroom, leaving a glum-faced Ada and Madame behind.

That night, a strange, muffled sound woke Ada from her sleep.

She crept down the hallway and peeked between the banister rails to see better. Below, her mother's hands were pressed to her face to hide her tears. The sound of her sobs echoed up the stairs into Ada's own heart. Two servants rushed into the hallway below, and Ada scurried out of sight.

"Lord Byron is dead."

"No!"

"Yes."

"Shall I wake Miss Byron?"

"No. Lady Byron says the girl is not to be told."

Ada retreated to her room. She closed the door and climbed back into bed, pulling the covers up under her chin. She lay there for some time, trying to decide how she felt about her father's death.

The next morning her mother said nothing at breakfast. Ada didn't either, but made sure to be extra polite. Before excusing herself for her lessons, she stood on tiptoe and planted the softest kiss she could on her mother's cheek. Ada thought she saw her mother's eyes grow wet, but Annabella waved her away.

Ada heard Madame calling her to start the first lesson of the day, but she walked in the opposite direction to the far end of the house. There, hung a portrait covered by a green velvet curtain. Ada had never been allowed to look at the portrait, nor had she found the courage to defy her mother. But today was different. She took a deep breath and pulled back the curtain to see her father's face for the very first time.

Her father's clear blue eyes looked just like the ones that peered back at her when she saw herself in the mirror. He wore a heavy red robe embroidered in gold and seemed to be listening to someone speaking just outside the painting's frame.

People claimed Lord Byron was one of the finest poets in England, possibly the world.

He didn't look like a poet, thought Ada. He looked more like an adventurer, or the sea captain she'd always imagined him to be. Ada tilted her head and folded an arm, mimicking his pose exactly.

Ada understood that her father was special. She knew he had written ideas that people talked about for a long time. Well, if he was extraordinary, then she must be, too. Satisfied, she let the curtain fall and headed to the schoolroom.

CHAPTER TWO

A da sat in the library, a finger to her lips in concentration. She studied the chessboard in front of her before moving a black knight. Then she got up and moved to the chair opposite. She examined the board again, then decisively moved the white queen.

"Checkmate," she announced to the room, empty except for Puff who was stretched out across the sofa.

Ada looked over at the cat. "You could at least be happy for me, Puff. That's the third game I've won in a row."

Puff yawned.

In the next room, Annabella was interviewing yet another tutor. The week before, Ada had been caught with a book of fairy stories hidden inside her workbook. So the last Madame had been dismissed for being careless with Ada's education.

Ada crept across the room and put her ear to the door to listen.

" . . . I could teach her *some* mathematics, I suppose," a man's voice was saying. "But it would have to be limited. There is only so much a female brain can manage."

"In that case, I shall not waste your time," Annabella replied in a tone Ada knew meant her mother was not pleased at all.

Ada was not sorry to hear the man go. She was ten now and felt she could learn plenty without a tutor. She was working her way through the books in their home library as fast as she could. Gobblebook, Ada called it, to describe the feeling of hungrily devouring every delicious word until she was full.

The characters in books were the closest people Ada had to friends. She had Mistress

Puff of course. But without other children in the house, she was often lonely. Ada wanted someone she could play with and someone to tell her marvelous ideas. She had no one like that . . . yet.

~

The next morning, Ada's mother summoned her earlier than usual. Annabella stood beside a woman Ada had not met before. The woman wore a plain black dress with a white collar, her smooth brown hair was parted in the middle and tucked into a sensible bun.

"Ada," Annabella said. "This is Miss Charlotte Stamp, your new governess. She will be responsible for your education and will travel with us to Europe later this year."

Ada curtseyed and tried not to look doubtful. Even the meanest tutors usually appeared eager to meet the daughter of the famous Lord Byron at first. Miss Stamp seemed friendly, but Ada was sure it was only a matter

of time before a scowl replaced the governess'
welcoming expression.

"It's a pleasure, Miss Byron." Miss Stamp
smiled. "We'll begin our lessons tomorrow.
But would you be so kind as to play chess with
me this afternoon?"

Well. This is new, Ada thought.

~

"Miss Stamp, I must warn you. I'm frightfully
good," Ada said as she set up the chessboard later
that afternoon.

"That's wonderful news, Miss Byron. I enjoy
a challenge."

They both turned their heads toward a mewling
sound. Puff sat on the arm of the floral sofa,
looking rather grumpy. Ada knew the cat did not
enjoy unexpected visitors in her personal lounge.

Miss Stamp held out her hand toward Puff, and
to Ada's astonishment, Puff licked Miss Stamp's
hand and settled into her lap.

"Your mother has gone over your lesson schedule with me," said Miss Stamp as they started to play. "Tell me, how else do you pass the time?"

"I love music," said Ada. "I could play the violin for hours. And I love dancing and reading." She paused before saying the next part. "I . . . I especially like fairy stories or adventure tales but Mama doesn't approve of those."

"Well, I am not required to report on *every* single book you read." Miss Stamp examined the board and moved another piece. "Do we also need to make time for letter writing or visits from your friends?"

Ada sighed as she took her turn. "I haven't got any. I write to my mother's friends sometimes. I tried writing to my cousin once, but he never wrote back."

"It is my experience, Miss Byron, that a person has many companions in a lifetime. Some understand your words and meaning perfectly.

And the others . . . . Well, it's often best to save your words for the ones who appreciate them the most. And there. Checkmate."

"Oh!" was all Ada could say. The governess had stunned her to silence.

"Newcomer's luck," Miss Stamp said breezily. "I shouldn't be saying this to a rival player, but I noticed that I played much better when I studied math at school. Something about working through all those problems sharpened my mind."

Ada turned this idea over as she glanced at her abandoned math workbook.

"Given that I can't stand up at the moment," Miss Stamp said, gesturing at Puff snoozing in her lap, "shall we play again?"

Ada nodded and turned back to the board, determined to win.

~

Miss Stamp was a wonder. She encouraged Ada to imagine far off places in geography. She made mathematics lessons fun. She told fairy tales in French, and danced Ada around the room for exercise. She listened patiently to Ada's stories, too, knowing just the right time to speak and when to be quiet. After so much loneliness, having a true friend living right in the house felt better than Ada could have possibly imagined. Even Puff was better behaved when Miss Stamp was around.

"How are you and Miss Stamp getting on, Ada?" her mother asked a few weeks later.

"Oh, Mama," she replied dreamily. "Miss Stamp is not just a governess. She's . . . an enchantress."

CHAPTER THREE

On a nice spring day, Miss Stamp sat in the shade of an oak tree with a book on her lap. The brim of her hat dipped occasionally, and Ada was sure she was dozing. Ada tossed her own book aside and flopped onto the blanket. She turned her face to the sky and stretched out her arms as if preparing to gather a cloud in her embrace.

What a joy their trip abroad had been! Ada thought back to all the places she'd seen. In Italy, Ada had set up her easel each morning on the balcony. She sketched the graceful archways of a palace and the distant sparkling turquoise sea. In Switzerland, Ada, Annabella, and Miss Stamp sailed on Lake Geneva, where their guide pointed out a vine-covered building on the shore.

"Have you ever heard of Lord Byron, the famous English poet?" the man asked, causing Ada to suppress a giggle. "He stayed there once!"

Ada could have traveled forever. She imagined sailing the world as a lady pirate, like the Irish queen Grace O'Malley. But after fifteen months, her mother was exhausted and wanted to return to England.

Annabella rented a house in the English countryside, hoping the air would restore her health. But it didn't seem to be working. She was away yet again at a spa she hoped might cure her tiredness.

Though the journey had exhausted her mother, it energized Ada. The world was so much bigger, brighter, and noisier than she had dreamed, the opposite of this quiet, isolated life in the

countryside. She rolled onto her belly and reached for her pencil and paper.

Dearest Mama,
Puff is a naughty cat and has got a little hiding
place in the chimney of my room where she puts
the birds she catches. She leaves them there until
she is hungry. This morning she dragged one
of them under my bed. I could hear her crunch
each bone.

Ada sighed. During the trip, she'd written a swashbuckling story about murder and ghosts. Mistress Puff's snacking habits were boring in comparison.

Ada stared up at the clouds, which looked like foamy waves on a windy day at sea. A pack of swallows swooped overhead. How graceful they were, soaring through the sky. The birds reminded her of a flying machine she'd heard about in Italy. Nobody had tried to build it yet, but the drawings she'd seen made clear that it was possible. All it would take was imagination and a good workspace.

Ada sat up.

"Miss Stamp!" She reached out to shake the boot of her sleeping guardian. "Miss Stamp!"

When her governess woke, Ada explained her new project in detail.

"I see," nodded Miss Stamp. "And what, may I ask, is your goal?"

"To fly."

"Right. In that case, we'd better get to work."

~

Days later, Ada and Miss Stamp stood disheveled yet proud as they looked at their new flying room in the barn. Piles of saddles and trunks had been dragged outside to clear the floor. Ropes dangled from the ceiling.

"For flight practice," Ada explained when the stable boy looked at her in confusion.

"Are you absolutely sure you're ready?" Miss Stamp asked as she tied two ropes to Ada's leather belt.

"Completely." Ada fixed a determined look on her face. She took a deep breath, ran a few steps forward, lifted her feet off the ground, and . . .

Crash. She tumbled forward out of the belt onto the floor.

"Think, Ada," Miss Stamp encouraged as she helped her up. "You've seen birds fly. What do they have that you don't?"

Ada pictured the gulls she saw gliding over Lake Geneva and the thrushes that landed on her windowsill in the springtime. They pushed the air away from their bodies as they rose, then their feathers caught the wind like sails to soar.

"Of course!" Ada exclaimed with a laugh. "Wings!"

Dear Mama,

I think I'll make wings out of silk. If that doesn't work, I'll try feathers. I am going to take the exact pattern of a bird's wing and then make a human-size pair. And if I fail, I have a back-up plan. Two of them, actually.

Your affectionate carrier pigeon,

AA Byron

My Dear Mama,

My wings are coming along nicely. Once I have figured out how to fly, I have a new idea. I'm going to build a mechanical horse with a steam engine inside. It will have giant wings big enough to carry it in the air, while a person (preferably me) rides on its back. There are still some equations to work out, but I think I can do it. The weather has been terrible. I have not been feeling well lately.

Your pigeon,

AA Byron

Ada sat on the floor of the flying room with paper, silk, and pages of measurements spread out around her. The wings had felt heavier than usual against her back that morning. She'd been sick all week with a fever she couldn't shake. At Miss Stamp's request she had stayed in bed the day before, but she was eager to finish her invention before her mama came home.

A shadow darkened the doorway.

"Ada! What is this?" Annabella asked.

"Mama!" Ada struggled to her feet. "You're home! Come, let me show you my wings."

"Wings? Flying? Ada, your letters hardly made sense. What's happened to your lessons?"

"Don't you see, Mama? I've almost got it worked out. If I can just figure out the right angle to attach the wings—"

"You will do no such thing. You have spent more than enough time on this flying nonsense."

"It is not nonsense! It's a brilliant idea. Just ask Miss Stamp, we've been working together—"

"You won't be any longer!" her mother snapped. Her voice was a tiny bit softer as she began again: "I have just spoken to Miss Stamp, Ada. She is engaged to be married. She will be leaving us soon."

Ada's knees felt weak. The walls seemed to spin around her and an unpleasant sweat broke out on her skin.

"Ada?"

I've never seen Mama look so frightened, Ada thought.

Then she fell to the floor and thought nothing else.

CHAPTER FOUR

Burning. The feeling of fire dancing on her skin. Somewhere a window was open, but the pain of the light was too much to bear. Ada turned away from it.

"We should bleed her," a voice drifted in from the hallway.

"You will do no such thing," said another.

They could not be speaking about her. She had no blood. She had no body. She was a bird flying over the rooftops, too high to be reached by sound or pain.

Slowly, an awareness came back to Ada's body and mind. She wriggled her fingers and toes and a face swam into view. It was a beautiful face, full of love.

"Mama," she whispered.

"Hush, my darling," her mother murmured, and placed her hand against her cheek.

Ada turned her head toward the cool palm and slept.

~

One misty day, a nurse pushed Ada in her wheelchair along the southern bank of the River Thames. Ada shivered under the wool blankets tucked around her.

"Do you want to go inside, miss?" the nurse asked.

"No, thank you," Ada replied quickly. "I'd much rather be outdoors."

It had been two years since Ada collapsed. She was now fifteen years old. There were no more flying experiments, and her laboratory in the barn had been dismantled. Ada and her mother had moved closer to the hospital in London. They lived in a house called the Limes, which

made Ada dream of fruit trees blooming under a
blue summer sky.

The London sky looked as dull and smudgy as
pencil scribbles, and the north side of the river
was tangled with weeds and leafless branches.
Ada pulled the shawl around her more tightly and
watched a lone steamer boat chop across the water.

Ada had come down with a terrible case of the

measles, her mother explained later. She'd been
semi-blind and unable to move her arms or legs.
When the illness faded, her doctors insisted she
remain in bed as her body healed.

Ada winced as the wooden wheelchair
bumped over a crack in the paving stones. The
old Ada would have been furious at her life now.
This new version of herself had no strength to

argue. Still, she would never miss a chance to see the sky. She closed her eyes and turned her face upward as a drizzling rain began to fall.

~

Later Ada would look back and marvel at how quickly her health fell apart and how long it took to put it back together. But heal she did, little by little. The first time she walked without help, she felt triumphant. The first time she was able to mount a horse and ride across the yard, she nearly cried with happiness.

She sometimes thought fondly of her flying experiments with Miss Stamp. But she did not long for them as she had in the first days of her illness. At seventeen, Ada's studies now felt like important work, not a schoolgirl's games. She knew now that time was precious.

A man tapped on her forehead, bringing her back to the present moment.

"Hmmm. The bone here indicates a great

deal of intelligence. But here," he continued, pressing gently above her ears. "Here, it is of a particularly stubborn and willful kind."

"I could have told you that and saved us the trouble," Ada muttered under her breath.

"Ada, hush," Annabella hissed.

The man seemed sure of himself as he looked at Ada. "Miss Byron, phrenology cannot be rushed. Thanks to the great men of science, we now understand that one's personality can be understood simply from the shape of the skull."

Ada tried not to roll her eyes.

When he left, Ada glared at her mother. "Finally, I am well enough to do whatever I wish, and you're wasting my time with this nonsense!"

"Phrenology is not nonsense, Ada. It's science."

"The power of steam is science. The curve and color of a rainbow is science. This fool tapping my skull is just silly. Now if you'll excuse me, I have work to do," Ada said, exasperated.

"You are not excused. And you may *not* speak to me that way. I am your mother!"

"I'm not a child!"

"You are *not* an adult yet. You need to understand more of what the world is like before stepping out into it. To that end, you will be going on a trip next week."

Ada perked up, imagining mountains and museums and a relaxing vacation from her mother's piercing gaze.

"Where am I going?"

"Northern England."

Annabella did not elaborate, but instead fixed Ada with a look that said the journey was not up for discussion.

"With me."

CHAPTER FIVE

To Ada, the trip to Northern England felt endless. She and her mother sweated through a tour of the blazing hot kilns at a pottery factory. Then they visited a ribbon company and listened to an explanation of silk-making that went on for so long Ada's eyelids started to droop. A jab in the ribs from Annabella's spear-sharp elbow woke her right up.

They finally came to a fabric factory.

"How much cloth do you produce each year?" Annabella asked the manager. She leaned in closer to hear his reply over the noise of the machinery.

Ada had absolutely no interest in the amount of fabric produced here or anywhere else, but tried to look engaged as she followed them into a dim hallway.

They walked by a room of men who sat at wooden desks, with piles upon piles of paper beside them, waiting for processing. Ada heard some of them murmur to themselves as they counted aloud.

"What are they doing?" Ada asked, glad to be away from the banging, clanging machines.

"Computing this year's profits," said the floor manager. He quickly shut the door. "Wouldn't want to disturb their calculations. Distracted computers make more mistakes!"

Ada looked through another door where workers punched holes into large cards. "And what do those pieces of paper do?"

"The holes in the cards give the machines directions. Come along, now. I'll show you how it all works."

Ada and her mother followed the manager into the mill. Workers stooped over long wooden frames laced with threads that twisted until cloth formed below. Ada knew these machines were looms.

"If you come this way, Lady Byron and Miss Byron," the manager continued, "you'll see our newest addition: a Jacquard loom."

Even if Ada had sat on her mother's shoulders, the wooden loom would have towered above them. Lengths of thread ran across the machine from two different directions: one like a waterfall and the other like a river.

Operators fed a long stretch of punched cards into the machine from the top. On the older looms, weavers were moving the threads by hand to make fabric. But with the Jacquard loom, the holes in the cards told the machine what patterns to weave.

"The cards give the machine instructions, and it does the rest on its own?" Ada asked.

"Exactly! It used to take two people an entire day just to weave a centimeter of fabric. But by

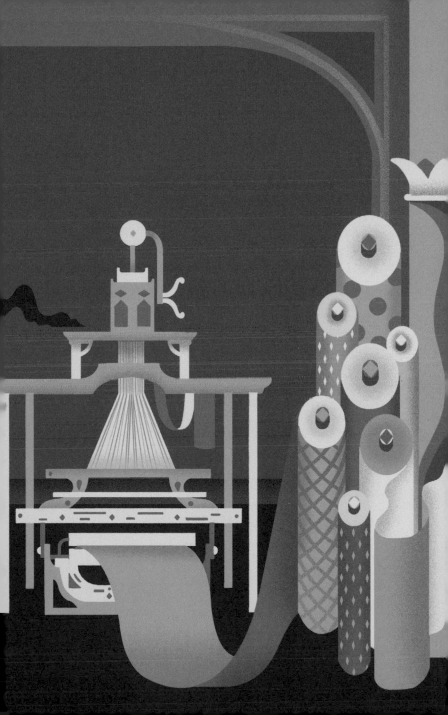

feeding punch cards into this machine, a single loom can create a meter of cloth in the same amount of time!"

"That's brilliant!" Ada exclaimed. She walked around the loom, examining it from every angle. The finished fabrics were works of art, with delicate flowers and birds shimmering against a silken background. This process, as Ada saw it, was science. The whole machine relied on precise calculations to determine the relationship between the card, the threads, and the machine. It was as if her mathematical exercises were coming to life, turning mechanics into magic.

As they left the factory, Ada turned to Annabella and uttered something she couldn't have imagined saying just hours before: "Thank you, Mama, for bringing me here."

~

From Northern England, Ada and Annabella took the train to King William and Queen

Adelaide's summer palace. Now that Ada was seventeen, it was time for her to meet the lords and ladies of the royal court. There would be a fancy ceremony and dinner, followed by a ball. Ada was dreading it, but Annabella was delighted to be among her old friends again.

Alone in her room, Ada looked at her dress of white tulle and satin. She tried to picture the delicate cloth rising from one of the looms in the loud, steaming factory, but she couldn't.

She tried to imagine herself wearing the dress. But she couldn't imagine that either.

In her mind, Ada ran through the steps she'd practiced night after night under Mama's watchful eye. First, a slow, dignified walk toward the thrones. Second, a low, graceful curtsey. Third, a quick prayer that she didn't topple over before it was time to rise.

It was important to make a good impression before the king and queen, of course. But Ada knew this visit was really about finding a husband.

Most girls her age were being matched up. Plenty of men would be interested in the daughter of the famous Lord Byron, not to mention the small fortune she would one day inherit.

The challenge, Ada thought, *will be finding a husband who understands me.*

To her surprise, the evening passed in a happy blur. Ada approached the king and queen, curtsied without so much as a wobble, then danced the night away. Annabella was invited to sit beside the queen at dinner where the two chatted warmly. There were occasional stares from people trying to catch a glimpse of Lady Byron and Ada.

"That's that mad poet's daughter!" one batty-looking lady said to a friend behind her fan. The woman thought she was whispering, but it was loud enough to reach Ada's ears. But Ada was too busy dancing and laughing to care.

At the end of the night, Ada and her mother giddily climbed into the carriage, exhausted

but excited. They could still hear the music drifting out of the Royal Pavilion as their carriage sped away.

"Did you enjoy yourself, Ada?"

"I did! The music was divine. I'd love to try playing the harp. I must say, though, that the party wasn't as interesting as the mathematics lecture we went to last month."

"And did you meet any interesting people this evening?"

"No," Ada confessed. "I hardly remember who I spoke to. But I did talk to your friend Mary Somerville, and she invited me over to discuss geometry next week."

Ada was surprised to see her mother's eyes linger on her face, as if it were that of a person she had not seen in some time.

"Your father used to call me the Princess of Parallelograms." Annabella's voice took on a gentle tone that Ada hadn't heard before.

"Really? What else did he used to say?"

Ada's question snapped Lady Byron out of her memories. "Never you mind," she replied, with a quick rap on her daughter's hand. Yet her voice was softer than usual, and her hand rested there for a moment, holding Ada's.

CHAPTER SIX

A woman with rosy cheeks and kind eyes opened the door to a tall brick house. To Ada's shock, she wore a bright orange robe wrapped around her dress.

"Miss Byron!" the lady exclaimed. "Do come in."

Ada had been looking forward to this visit with her mother's old friend, Mary Somerville, for a long time. Mary's scientific papers and books were some of the most respected in Europe. Since she couldn't be called a "*man* of science," like almost all of England's top researchers, a reviewer of her last paper invented a new word to describe her: *scientist.*

"It's wonderful that your mother has urged you toward mathematics and the sciences," Mary said as they sat down to tea. "My own parents feared that the strain of mathematics was too much for the female brain. I had to sneak a small candle under the covers at bedtime and read in secret. They're lucky I didn't accidentally burn the house down." Mary took a sip of tea, her eyes smiling at Ada over the rim of her cup.

"Mama hopes I will take a husband soon. I must say, I hate the idea. I suppose I'll have to give up my studies."

"But Miss Byron, why do you speak as though your marriage and your studies are two separate things that cannot coexist? I got married. I had two children. *And* I continued my work. There is no need to choose between a family life and a life of the mind. Those who think there is probably don't have much of the second."

That night, Ada sat down with a book of geometry, the kind of math that focuses on shapes. She traced lines and angles in her notebook. The pages flew by one after the other until daybreak.

Ada wrote to Mary nearly every day, asking questions about equations in her workbook. The letters that came back gave answers in clear, simple language. Though Mary knew more than Ada, her explanations felt more like listening to a friend than a lecture.

"Miss Byron, there's someone I would like you to meet," Mary said during Ada's next visit. "A great mathematician and first-rate inventor called Charles Babbage is having a gathering. You *must* attend as my guest."

"Must I, Mrs. Somerville? Parties can be so dull."

"Not this one, Miss Byron. I think you'll find this one most fascinating."

~

A week later, the carriage pulled up in front of a brick house with brightly lit windows. The sound of countless voices tumbled out onto the street. Unlike the quiet dinners Ada often attended with her mother, this house seemed to crackle with energy.

"Miss Byron!" Mary called from across the room. Ada squeezed through the crowd to her friend and warmly kissed her cheeks. "Miss Byron, allow me to introduce you to our host this evening, Mr. Charles Babbage."

A man in a rumpled coat with messy hair stood before her. "It's a pleasure to meet you, Mr. Babbage."

"Welcome, Miss Byron. Mrs. Somerville tells me you're interested in mathematics?"

"I am. She has been so kind as to tutor me in geometry. I cannot yet match her skill, but it's not for lack of trying. You're an inventor?"

Charles directed Ada's attention to a small glass case, where a mechanical doll balanced a bird on her tiny outstretched fingers. He turned a crank, and the doll bowed from inside her case. "This is the Silver Lady . . . "

But Ada's attention had drifted to an object on a wooden table behind the inventor. Half-obscured by a curtain was a machine unlike any Ada had ever seen: a three-foot high tower of brass tubes, wheels, gears, and cogs.

"What's that machine?" Ada leaned to one side to see it more clearly.

Charles stepped back to give her a better view. "Ah, this is my favorite invention. I call it the Difference Engine. This is only a small section of it. I've had some, er, trouble having the whole machine built. But this part should be enough to demonstrate."

Charles made some careful adjustments to the wheels in the tower, then grasped the crank on the top of the machine and pushed it back and forth. Metal cogs began to click and turn below.

"When it's up and running, the machine will be able to count numbers up to ten thousand and add and multiply large numbers, all without any silly little mistakes that humans make!"

Ada said nothing, too distracted by the wonder before her eyes. She thought of the human computers in the factory she'd seen, counting money, tracking expenses, and checking each other's work all day long. With this machine, they could solve math problems with half the time and ink!

She knelt down to peer at the fine grooves on the wheels. Each was numbered in bold black script. Ada had to fight the urge to pry each gear from the next so she could better understand how the machine worked.

"Others have tried to build calculating machines, of course," said Charles. "But no one's ever made one that didn't require a person's help at every step. But my machine is *entirely* automatic. All you have to do is turn the handle, and the engine does the work."

"Is it right to call it a thinking machine?" Mary asked, peering at it curiously.

"It's not actually thinking," Ada said thoughtfully. "A person still has to enter the numbers. This machine is simply doing the work of sorting out the answer."

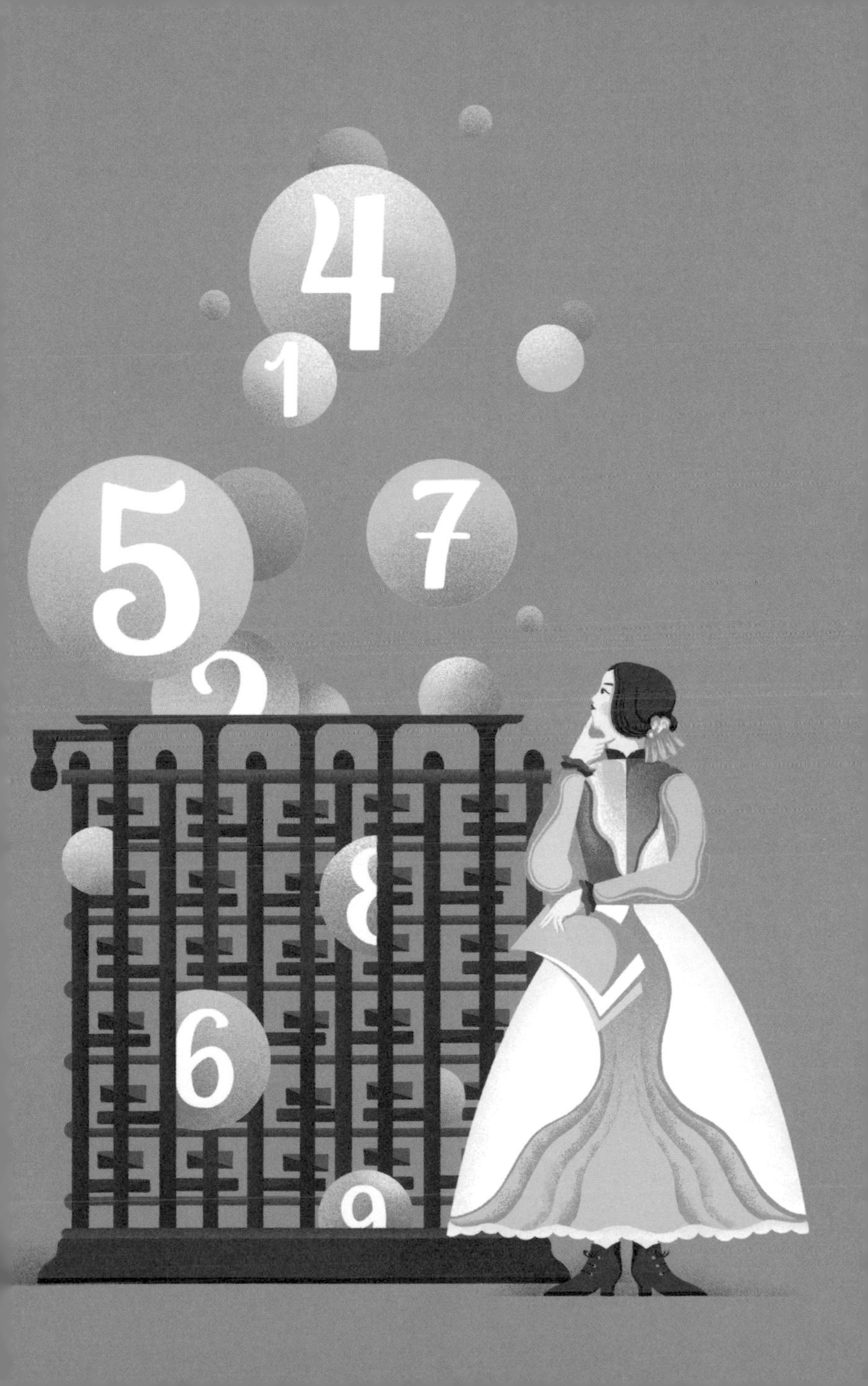

Charles looked at Ada, blinking in surprise that she had understood his Difference Engine so well. "That's correct, Miss Byron."

"When will it be finished?" she asked, unable to take her eyes off the machine.

"Who knows," Charles said, shrugging. "My foolish engineer quit, and the British government won't fund it."

"You're not giving up, are you?" Ada looked up in alarm.

"Never," Charles replied with a wink. "Though there are many people who would be relieved if I did."

CHAPTER SEVEN

A da sat at her harp, practicing her favorite song. As she struck each chord, she imagined the sound as its own shape floating from the strings into the air and dancing above her head. She thought a lot about music these days and even more about Charles Babbage's machine. It was as if the clicking wheels of the Difference Engine were now spinning in her own mind, working through a problem whose solution would be more exciting than any she had found before.

There was a knock at the door. A footman appeared holding a silver tray piled with letters and invitations. Ada noticed her name scrawled in unfamiliar handwriting and plucked it from the pile. She read it quickly, and immediately seized a pen from the desk to write back, happily accepting Charles Babbage's invitation to join him for tea.

~

"Good Lord, doesn't he have a housekeeper?" Ada's mother whispered as they stepped into Charles's parlor. In the light of day, the inventor's house looked far more suited to science experiments than fancy parties. Sketches and drawings cluttered the tables. Even more crumpled pieces of paper were strewn across the floor.

Ada was disappointed to see the Difference Engine sitting unchanged on its table. She asked Charles whether he'd made progress on it since they'd last met.

"No, no, of course not." Charles waved Ada's question away. "I suspect I'll be working on it forever. No, I've set it aside for now. Another idea has come to me, one that makes my

Difference Engine look dull by comparison. Look." He picked a sheet of crumped paper off the carpet and smoothed it out on the table.

Ada wasn't sure what she was looking at. Babbage's drawings were sloppy, his handwriting nearly unreadable. But she thought she could make out a diagram of a new machine.

"What on earth is that, Mr. Babbage?" Annabella asked skeptically.

"It's my greatest idea yet." Charles's face shone with excitement. "The Difference Engine can calculate mathematical tables, certainly. But this machine can do far more. I call it the Analytical Engine. It will be the size of a small train. I'll need several thousand cogwheels, I'm not sure just how many yet, and it will be controlled by a series of punch cards—"

"Like the Jacquard loom!" Ada blurted out. She could still picture the amazing machine in the loud textile mill.

"Exactly! And with the punch cards, the number of operations the engine can perform are limited only to the number of cards we can create. Every calculation will be performed the same way, every time. It has excited me more than any other project! It feels like I'm walking across a bridge from the known world to an unknown one. I have no idea what I'll find once I'm there, but I am curious about where the path will lead."

~

Later, when Ada and her mother were at home, Annabella wrinkled her nose in disapproval. "Mr. Babbage is a brilliant man, and I agree that his Difference Engine is an intriguing and highly practical machine. But this Analytical Engine doesn't make sense. Babbage himself doesn't seem to know how it works."

"That's what makes it exciting! It's the seed of an idea. I don't blame him for not being able to think about anything else," Ada replied.

"Is that because your thoughts are consumed with it as well?" Annabella asked with a raised eyebrow. "Ada, I am pleased to see your progress in math, and delighted by your friendship with Mrs. Somerville. But it's time to turn your thoughts to your future. To marriage."

"Marriage to whom, exactly? That man you had me sit next to at that one dinner party—Lord What's-His-Name? I talked about math to him for nearly forty-five minutes, and he hardly said a word. I'm not sure he even knew what geometry was. And that awful ball the week before . . . I asked every dance partner his favorite equation, and not one had a decent answer. Can you imagine spending a lifetime with someone like that?"

"It is possible that, over the course of a lifetime, you'll find something to talk about other than numbers." Annabella had the hint of a smile on her lips. "There is a ball next week, Ada. A gentleman will be present that you should meet.

Mrs. Somerville herself has invited you, and I've written to accept the invitation on your behalf."

Ada took a deep breath. It was something she'd learned long ago to stop her from saying something she might regret. "Very well, Mother," she said.

~

The ball was as dull as Ada imagined. The hostess, Lady Philips, looked disapprovingly at Ada's dress, and Ada noticed how she emphasized the "Byron" part of her name in each introduction. It was as though Ada was only worth talking to because of her famous father.

Ada hid a yawn of boredom behind her fan. If the ball ended early enough, she might be able to finish the problem she'd been working on at home.

Lady Philips approached, practically dragging a young man behind her. "Miss Byron, may I introduce you to Lord William King?"

"Just 'William' will do." William bent to kiss Ada's hand, and she blushed. The face that looked back at her when he lifted his head was quite nice to look at.

"It is a pleasure to meet you, Miss Byron. Lady Philips tells me that you are interested in mathematics. I am as well, although a different sort. I am interested in architecture. I appreciate the curves of an arch all the more when I can work out the calculations behind it. Sometimes during services at my church, I'm distracted trying to understand the angles of the steeple. It's an odd hobby, I know."

"Not odd at all," said Ada.

"It's a beautiful church," William went on. "I would love to show it to you one day."

Ada met his eyes and smiled. "I think I might like that very much."

The next morning Ada sat with a blank piece of paper and a nervous feeling in the pit of her stomach. She tapped her fingers on the desk, wrote a few lines, then scratched them out, and crumpled the paper, hurling it toward the fireplace. She reached for a fresh sheet of paper, took a deep breath, and tried again.

Dear Lord King,
I thought to myself after we met last night how few young men would talk with so much feeling about their country church. I admire your enthusiasm.

She moved on to the next line before she lost her nerve.

It was the first of many letters Ada wrote to William, who replied kindly and thoughtfully. He seemed to remember every detail, asking about her health if she mentioned having a cold, or if she'd enjoyed a lecture she was planning to attend. He shared details of life in his countryside home as well, until it felt as familiar to her as a place she'd already been. By the time he wrote to invite her for a horseback ride on his estate, Ada could see herself living alongside him there.

Ada went for her visit and when they returned from their horseback ride, her cheeks were pink and shining. William had asked her a very important question. Ada had said yes.

~

Two months later, Ada stepped into the drawing room at her mother's home wearing a dress of cream silk. Annabella quietly wiped away tears, but Ada noticed only William, standing by the priest at the front of the room. She walked carefully toward him.

"The rings, please," the priest said.

Ada heard a tinkling sound behind her and turned to look. There, sauntering up the aisle, was Puff with two gleaming gold rings dangling from a velvet ribbon around her neck.

CHAPTER EIGHT

"Are we finished yet?" asked Ada, stretching her aching shoulders. The painter peeked out from behind the canvas, a spare paintbrush clenched in her teeth, and shook her head.

Ada resumed her position, with her hand at her waist and her head turned to the side. She had a million things she'd rather be doing than standing for her portrait, like concentrating on the quadratic equations waltzing through her mind.

A crash came from down the hall—her eldest son, Byron, undoubtedly. The mess that boy could make never ceased to amaze her. The chattering voice of his little sister, Annabella, followed soon after. It was only a matter of time before baby Ralph began to cry.

"Lady Lovelace?" called the frazzled governess, sticking her head into the room.

It took a moment for Ada to realize that the woman was referring to her. William had only recently been made "The Earl of Lovelace." And her new title, "The Countess of Lovelace," sounded like an old person locked away in a

stuffy old tower. She supposed the name would grow on her.

The painter waved the governess away and shut the door. But the idea that had been forming in Ada's mind had dissolved into a jumble of random numbers. She sighed.

Life as a mother and wife left Ada less time for math than she'd hoped. Although she was taking a correspondence course in mathematics,

the children always seemed to demand her attention just when she'd started a particularly hard equation.

William was kind as always, but he'd become obsessed with renovating their country home. He was either buried in blueprints or dashing off to another meeting with his chief architect. This left the children and the care of their estate to Ada.

Worst of all, Mary Somerville was moving away to Italy. Ada could still write to her, but it would take forever to get responses to her questions. She was going to miss her friend and mentor terribly.

Ada loved William and her children, but she wanted a project to fully immerse herself in, the way she'd been obsessed with flying as a child, or the way Charles Babbage was obsessed with his engines.

Babbage! Of course! One of England's greatest unfinished inventions sat right in her friend Charles's living room. She could help him finish the Difference Engine, his brilliant calculating machine! Then, with that out of the way, he might start working on his Analytical Engine again, the even more mysterious invention he had explained to her years before.

She must write to him at once. Ada hurried off to her study, the velvet robe trailing behind her.

"Lady Lovelace! Lady Lovelace, come back!" the painter cried.

But Ada had already shut herself in her study.

~

"How is your work coming along, Lady Lovelace?"

"Very well. Thank you for asking, Mr. Babbage."

Since she'd walked out of her portrait session, Ada and Charles had been writing to one another regularly. Today, Ada had finally made the journey to visit him.

"I spent all week on this last problem you sent."

Babbage flipped through the pages she'd brought him. "You did well. I can't find a single flaw in your logic."

"When I sit down to study, I feel as if I could never be tired, like I could go on forever. But at the end of the day, I've accomplished barely half of what I set out to do." She laughed. "Now tell me, what's this issue you're having with the Difference Engine?"

"My problem, Lady Lovelace, is that—*gah!* Hang on."

Charles leapt from his chair and threw open his front door. "STOP THAT INFERNAL RACKET!" he bellowed into the street, where a surprised-looking organ grinder had started playing a tune.

"Street musicians," he grumbled, returning to his seat. "They're the bane of my existence. As I was saying, Lady Lovelace. My problem is that the scientific men of this country are fools. No one understands me, so no one will give me the money to finish my machine."

"You don't make things easy," Ada replied. "You did not attend that investment meeting. I also tried to introduce you to that newspaper editor. He might have written something encouraging about it."

"And have him bungle all the facts? No thank you."

"And then there was the prime minister . . . "

"Oh, that old—"

"You shouted at him, Mr. Babbage! Of course no one wants to pay for our . . . I mean *your* . . . machine if you're going to be so difficult about it."

Babbage set down his tea and rummaged around on his desk before pulling out a stack of bound papers.

"This might interest you, Lady Lovelace. A man in Switzerland has written an article about the Analytical Engine, and I'd like it to be published here in England. The only problem is that it's all in French. I need a translator. If I recall, your French is excellent."

Ada took the stack of papers from him eagerly. The article was many pages long, with diagrams she recognized as tidier versions of Babbage's sketches. She read aloud from the final paragraph, translating from the French: "Who can foresee the future uses of such an invention?"

"Ada, you understand my machine better than almost anyone," said Charles. "I'd like you to translate the article. But I'd also like you to help people understand what this machine has the power to do."

Ada flipped through the paper faster, her mind and heart racing. "How long do we have?"

"Six months."

"Six months! In that case, goodbye for now, Mr. Babbage. I have work to do."

CHAPTER NINE

B ack at home, Ada spread the pages of the article across her desk. The writer had done a good job describing the engine's workings. But his paper didn't talk about what was so thrilling about Babbage's new idea.

The Difference Engine, the machine Ada had seen on her first visit to Babbage's house, was fairly straightforward. Crank the handle, and solved equations came out.

The new machine was capable of so much more. The Analytical Engine could perform virtually any calculation, but beyond that it might be able to work with complex math problems, words, music notes, maybe even pictures. Ada understood how even educated people like her mother found the Analytical Engine difficult to understand. What they needed was someone to explain it to them in simple, everyday language, just as Mary Somerville had once explained geometry to her.

"It's not just a calculating machine," Ada muttered to herself, tapping her fingers on the desk. "The Analytical Engine weaves algebraic patterns, just as the Jacquard loom *weaves* flowers and leaves into cloth."

She grabbed her pen and started to write.

~

Back and forth the letters went. Ada's neighbors grew used to the sight of Lady Lovelace racing to catch the mail carrier's horse, with her skirts gathered in one hand and a letter in the other, flapping the envelope in the air to dry the ink. As the deadline drew nearer, Ada often joined Charles in his home and they sat together surrounded by notes and half-drunk cups of tea.

Ada pushed a pile of papers across the table toward Charles. "Here's the latest draft. I added the bit about using the machine to calculate Bernoulli numbers you asked for last time."

"Ah, excellent." Charles peered over his glasses as he flipped through the pages. "These are quite useful. I want people to appreciate the power this machine has for complex concepts."

"I've also added a few of my own theories." Ada pointed to a passage she'd written. "I firmly believe that the machine could work with *any* bit of information, like letters, words, or even musical notes. Can you imagine: a machine that understands the notes well enough to compose its own songs? What if it could create images, like a painter on canvas?"

"The Analytical Engine is a machine for *numbers*, Lady Lovelace," Charles countered, frowning and scribbling something out. "It's not for—"

"Mr. Babbage," Ada interrupted impatiently,

"math isn't just about how numbers relate to each other. It's about how *all* things relate to each other."

Babbage laughed, but Ada carried on. "It is! Everything is math: the arc of the sun in the sky, the distance between the stars, the way a family expands as children grow up and have children of their own. Those relationships are the *same*, no matter where in the world a person lives or what language they speak. It can't be a coincidence. It's science, but it's also poetry. It's poetical science! And this machine has the power to understand that language, even if *you* don't see it."

"I think you have too much imagination, Lady Lovelace," Charles chuckled.

"I think you don't have enough," she shot back.

Ada left feeling annoyed. Halfway down the street she spotted one of the street musicians she knew Charles loathed, and a mischievous grin spread across her face.

She handed the organ grinder a few coins and pointed to Charles's house. "Stand out front, play as loud as you can, and don't stop until you've finished the song, no matter what the gentleman inside says."

Then she walked toward the park feeling much better.

Ada got so wrapped up in her work that she rarely left her room, even for meals. William warned the children to keep their voices down outside their mother's study. One night, while going over her penciled diagrams in ink, she fell asleep with her cheek on the desk. When she woke the next morning, there was a blanket around her shoulders and a stack of diagrams finished in ink. William had completed them for her.

She finished just in time for the deadline. Her notes were more than twice as long as the original article. She flipped through her final draft and a sentence leapt out at her.

The Analytical Engine cannot create anything new, she had written. *It, however, can do whatever we program it to do.*

The machine could not generate any new ideas, it was true. But after this project, Ada knew for certain that *she* could.

Early one morning a few weeks later, Ada heard a thump outside and ran downstairs, flinging open the door.

There on the step was a parcel wrapped in brown paper. With shaking hands, she tore it open and read the first page.

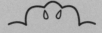

SKETCH
of the
Analytical Engine
Invented by
Charles Babbage, Esq.
With Notes by the Translator

Her name was absent, just as she had insisted. She knew that men would never take a scientific article seriously with a woman's name on the cover but she didn't care. Even if no one ever knew all she had done to bring this work into the world, *she* would know. She squeezed the package tight to her chest.

CHAPTER TEN

Once the paper was published, Ada thought offers of support for Charles's machine would flow in from scientists, politicians, and businessmen. Hopefully everyone would now understand the wonderful possibilities of the Analytical Engine and would be eager to fund it.

But the letters never came. Babbage's reputation as a difficult person to work with had traveled far and wide. Important people had come to know the inventor as a man who didn't finish the projects he started.

"The world needs this machine, William!" cried Ada pacing the floor of her office seething. "I refuse to let him sabotage himself. If he would just let me speak for him, I could convince people to help him build it."

"If anyone can convince Babbage to do this, darling, it's you. You know how stubborn you both . . . I mean, how stubborn *he* is," William said, ignoring a sharp look from his wife. "He might be too proud to agree, but it can't hurt to try."

~

Ada always wrote to Charles before she paid him a visit, but this time she marched right up to his door.

"Mr. Babbage!" called Ada, breezing past the dismayed housekeeper who had been in the middle of tidying up a mess of papers in the entryway. "I have something urgent to discuss with you."

Charles gave her a startled look.

"I have it all worked out," Ada began. "We're going to get this machine built."

"Lady Lovelace—"

"No, listen! William and I will find support for

your project. All you need to do is work out the mechanical issues."

"Lady Lovelace."

"We both know that dealing with people isn't your strong suit, Mr. Babbage. That's why we will make such a magnificent team! Your machine is incredible. It could change history. It could—"

"Lady Lovelace!" Charles almost shouted. There was a harsh note in his voice that Ada heard him use with others, but never before with her. He softened a little, as if catching himself, before he spoke again. "I appreciate your enthusiasm, Lady Lovelace, but I refuse your offer. And I must ask you never to speak of it again."

Disappointed, Ada stared at her friend. She noticed the creases in his forehead from countless hours squinting by candlelight over diagrams and brass cogs. Ada loved leaping to the next challenge. But her friend, she realized, was different. Perhaps Charles didn't *want* to build the machine. Perhaps he was afraid of being laughed at or criticized. Perhaps he wanted to stay daydreaming forever, in private, in his own home, with trusted friends.

Ada had spent a lifetime ignoring people's whispers and curiosity. It rarely bothered her when people made fun of her or stared as she walked into a room, but Babbage was not like her. And a good friend would not push him where he did not want to go.

"I will not speak of it again," Ada said gently.

~

Ada impatiently checked the clock at the train station. Charles was always late, and she was eager to enter the fair.

Eight years after their collaboration on the Analytical Engine paper, the mathematician and the inventor were even closer friends, which meant Charles had found even more ways to irritate her. Ada smiled as she spotted a familiar face and a rumpled coat making its way toward her through the station.

Poor Charles, Ada thought. She knew he was angry about not having been invited to display his work at the fair. (The organizers apparently found him too difficult.)

"These infernal crowds," he grumbled, as he reached her. "How great is this exhibition anyway?"

"The greatest. Now come on," she said, tucking her hand through his arm. "We're late!"

Ada had been looking forward to the exhibition for months. In the years since the article she'd translated was published, the world seemed to be changing faster than ever. New machines and technologies were being thought up for factories, fields, and hospitals. To showcase all these advancements, English royalty had organized a massive fair where inventors and scientists from all over the world could show off their work. It was called *The Great Exhibition of the Works of Industry of All Nations*, though everyone just referred to it as The Great Exhibition.

Ada gazed upon the magnificent glass exhibition hall with wonder. It was beautiful, decorated with statues and huge trees, planted to look as if they'd grown inside the building. Even better were rows upon rows of inventions that made Ada's mind spin. There were machines that made everything from envelopes to steel beams. A gigantic telescope brought previously unexplored parts of the sky into view. The latest version of the Jacquard loom stood in full view, and Ada circled it with fond memories swirling in her mind. But a new mechanical marvel quickly caught her attention.

"Look here, Charles, a steam-powered plow! It can replace the work of ten horses."

"What good is that?" Charles grumbled.

Ada thought about her diagrams for a steam-powered flying horse all those years ago and smiled. Then she stopped in her tracks, feeling a pain so sharp it took her breath away. She was only thirty-six years old but the pains seemed to be coming more and more often lately.

"Ada, are you all right?"

Catching her breath, Ada saw the look of concern on her friend's face and pushed aside her fears.

"It's nothing, Charles," she said. "Nothing at all. Now, come. Let's see what the future looks like."

Ada could not have predicted exactly what the digital age would look like when she penciled out what we now realize was the first published computer program. But her notes make clear that she understood, before almost anyone else, just how many possibilities the computing era could hold, even if she never got to see that future herself.

Ada Lovelace died of uterine cancer at her home in London on November 27, 1852. She was thirty-six years old, the same age as her father, Lord Byron, when he died. At Ada's request, she was buried next to him at the church near his childhood home.

Charles Babbage died in 1871. He never finished building the Difference Engine or the Analytical Engine. In the late 1990s, using Babbage's original plans, a team of computer scientists built a working model of the Difference Engine. You can see it today in London's Science Museum. One hundred years after Ada's death, Ada's fellow mathematicians rediscovered her work. They marveled at how a woman who had lived long before the age of computers had been able to imagine them and the immense potential they held to shape our world.

In the 1970s a group of computer scientists created a programming language for the U.S. Department of Defense. It's used around the world to power rockets, banks, trains, and airplanes. They named it after one of computing's earliest pioneers: Ada.

PUNCH CARD PUNCHLINE

Ada discovered that punch cards can use a series of punched-out symbols to give machines specific directions to complete tasks like weaving cloth or counting numbers. The symbols on the cards can be thought of as coding directions to the machine. Each letter below has been assigned a symbol. Use the card to decipher the code and discover the answer to the jokes below!

1. What do you get when you cross a cat with a parrot?

2. Where did Miss Stamp go to buy Ada's new chess set?

Turn to page 126 for the solutions!

PUNCH CARD ALPHABET

ADA SAYS!

A computer program is a set of instructions for a computer. A programming language is a set of symbols and rules for using those symbols that a computer can understand. Computers don't have to be electrical! A computer can be mechanical, like a loom, or even biological, like a person.

Let's say Ada came up with a programming language to give instructions to her cat, Mistress Puff. Grab a friend, and one of you will be the programmer (Ada) and the other will be the computer (Mistress Puff).

Here's the language:

↑   **Go forward one step**

→   **Turn to the right**

←   **Turn to the left**

○   **If there is anything in front of you, pick it up**

RULES

You can place a number in front of a symbol to tell Mistress Puff to repeat the symbol that many times. (Use a comma in between symbols!)

If you wrote your programming language down, it would look like this:

4↑, →, 6↑, ◯

(This means take 4 steps forward, turn to the right, take 6 steps forward, if there's anything in front of you pick it up.)

Now you try! Take turns being the programmer and computer, and even make up a few symbols of your own.

TALK LIKE A COMPUTER!

Modern computers don't use punch cards, letters, or symbols to communicate. (They use the numbers 1 and 0 instead.) Humans created a special language out of these numbers called "binary code," a language that only computers and programmers understand. See if you can decipher the message using 1s and 0s and become an ace programmer like Ada.

1. What was the name of the book Ada wrote about flying?

1000110 / 1001100 / 1011001 / 1001111 / 1001100 / 1001111 / 1000111 / 1011001

2. What were Ada's favorite childhood books about?

1000110 / 1000001 / 1001001 / 1010010 / 1001001 / 1000101 / 1010011

Turn to page 126 for the solutions!

BINARY ALPHABET

A	1000001	N	1001110
B	1000010	O	1001111
C	1000011	P	1010000
D	1000100	Q	1010001
E	1000101	R	1010010
F	1000110	S	1010011
G	1000111	T	1010100
H	1001000	U	1010101
I	1001001	V	1010110
J	1001010	W	1010111
K	1001011	X	1011000
L	1001100	Y	1011001
M	1001101	Z	1011010

W♀GRAMMER

We are proud to announce a collaboration with the organization Wogrammer. One of their journalism fellows wrote these activities for use in this volume.

Wogrammer is on a mission to break stereotypes and inspire more girls to pursue careers in STEM. Like Rebel Girls, the organization leads the charge in profiling diverse women, offering an authentic perspective while celebrating and showcasing their accomplishments.

Visit them at **www.wogrammer.org** or **@Wogrammer**

Solutions to "Punch Card Punchline"
1. **What do you get when you cross a cat with a parrot?** *A carrot!*
2. **Where did Miss Stamp go to buy Ada's new chess set?** *The pawn shop!*

Solutions to "Talk Like a Computer!"
3. **What was the name of the book Ada wrote about flying?** *Flyology*
4. **What were Ada's favorite childhood books about?** *Fairies*

ACKNOWLEDGEMENTS

We couldn't have created this series without the incredible women who inspire us. Ada Lovelace conceived of a future that many of us would not have predicted a few decades ago. We love her pioneering spirit!

Thank you Corinne Purtill for crafting such a beautiful tribute to a remarkable woman with humor and sensitivity. Thank you, Marina Muun, for creating beautiful illustrations. Monique Aimee, the cover lettering is gorgeous! And thank you to our brilliant copyeditors and proofreaders Susan Nicholson and Taylor Morris.

To Wogrammer, you rock! We are so grateful that Hillary Fleenor was able to bring these coding activities to life. Kathleen Ortiz, thank you for going to bat for this speedy collaboration.

And to the Rebel Girls of the world, we are nothing without YOU. Your support is what keeps us aiming higher and fighting harder. Keep resisting, keep pushing, keep creating!

ABOUT REBEL GIRLS

Rebel Girls is a cultural media engine on a mission to balance power and build a more inclusive world. It is best known for the wildly successful book *Good Night Stories for Rebel Girls*, a collection of one hundred tales of extraordinary women throughout history.

Good Night Stories for Rebel Girls, published in 2016, was an overnight sensation, becoming the most successful book in crowdfunding history. The title has since been released in over eighty-five territories around the world. Following the book's triumph, Rebel Girls released *Good Night Stories for Rebel Girls Volume 2* and *I Am a Rebel Girl: A Journal to Start Revolutions*. Good Night Stories for Rebel Girls is also a podcast, highlighting the lives of prominent women with beautiful sound design.